TRAPPED

A Collection of Short Stories

Author Redacted

Copyright © 2023 Author Redacted

All rights reserved

The characters and events are entirely fictitious. Any similarity to real persons, living or dead, is coincidental and not intended by the author.

No part of this book may be reproduced, or stored in a retrieval system, or transmitted in any form or by any means, electronic, mechanical, photocopying, recording, or otherwise, without express written permission from the author.

Breaking the Tension

Long Wake: Coffee Break

Queue Here, Please

Rook at Lovell Bank

Ditch

Roadman

Caught in a Moment

AUTHOR REDACTED

BREAKING THE TENSION

Before we start looking into the disturbing events at Cragforth, I believe that two indisputable facts must be clarified with regards to water in general:

1. Water has a surface tension that allows it to hold its shape and resist external forces due to the cohesive nature of the water molecules. There is an inward force that causes molecules to contract and hold on to each other, and a tangential force parallel to the surface of the liquid. This parallel force behaves like a net or a stretched membrane. This is what holds rain together in a droplet as it falls from the sky, or water into drops from a leaking tap. It is more complicated than this, of course, but for the purpose of this report, I believe this level of science will suffice. It explains why small insects can run across water without getting their toes wet (they are too light or spread their weight over too great an area to break the net) and so it appears that they can walk on water, or when Olympic swimmers are photographed as they rise out of the water and their heads are covered with water before the net breaks. There are some glorious photos of this online, and I recommend viewing them before reading this report.

2. Water remembers.

Cragforth Council's Community Swimming Pool was located at

the rear of the town's high school. It was built to provide both school children and the wider community access to safe swimming waters to learn in as the town itself was surrounded by several large bodies of waters that regularly claimed the lives of locals and visitors over many years.

There were ponds of various sizes in the woodlands that surrounded the town, as well as a lake that curved round the town in a pleasing crescent moon. A little further out, the quarry that had been mined for generations had been filled with water to make the eyesore more palatable. The deep waters were enticing, though it was often said that the runoff burned and the dark waters were not dark for lack of light. More than once, environmentalists had called for the clean up of the area after runoff water had been tested and found to fail safety standards.

A small river ran north of the town and spilled out into the bay through the sands to the west. It once turned a waterwheel, but it had been strangled down to barely more than a dribble, a far cry from its heyday as a wide and roaring river. Now there was not even enough water to raise small boats or canoes. The locals took to racing rubber ducks in an annual tradition to raise money for various charities, church rooves, community pantries and the like. The ducks would be collected at the end of the race and saved for the next time. Very few ducks made it past the safety net that was installed at the finish line, though occasionally the odd plastic duck made it to freedom. Provided the day was dry, even if overcast, hundreds would turn out onto the sandy banks to watch and cheer on their rubber duck. People were always cautious though, especially with small children wandering too close to the edge, as there was always the risk of the high sand banks collapsing and dropping them into the quick water and the quicksand below.

A canal ran north to south through the town, bisecting it. In centuries past, the canal had been a lifeline for commerce before the train station arrived (The train line caused its own problems, though these were seldom due to water). More recently the canal, and specifically its pub at the lock, were used by outsiders as they paused on their narrowboat holidays, and the occasional tourist boat that served afternoon tea whilst customers watched the scenery, which in itself was not wholly unattractive. In winter though, the canal's waters dipped below freezing, and being so near to a pub whose doors opened onto the towpath, if the landlord was not careful, his regulars occasionally took a long dip.

A water treatment facility, locally known as the 'new sewage', worked well, for the most part, in cleaning the water and removing toxins, chemicals and debris before allowing the treated water to run off into the sea. 'New sewage' replaced 'old sewage', the town's original sewage system from the mid-Victorian 'grand build' (heralded in its day), that collected both sewage and rainwater. The town grew, as towns often do, and 'old sewage' was no longer fit for purpose. The town ran out of money quickly due to the number of beach-cleans it needed to do each year, until finally a loan was facilitated to update the entire town's sewage system. Locals suspected this was because the sewage affected the more profitable towns along the seafront and their holiday homes that required pristine beaches.

Cragforth had many bodies of water, each with their own particular dangers, so it had been decided the town, even one as small as this, required its own community swimming pool to ensure that all could learn to swim in safety.

There were two points of access to the swimming pool; one through the high school itself, down a long corridor and through a small door that was kept locked from the school side. The second entrance was a larger door that was open to the public and was accessible down a small path from the main road.

The pool was built purely for function. It was only 25 metres long (a whopping 82ft), and barely 5m wide (16ft). The shallow end was around 60cm (2ft) deep, and if someone tall stood in the deep end with a snorkel, they would breathe quite comfortably. There were no diving boards; this was strictly by design of the original committee who didn't want to encourage that sort of behaviour in nature, and diving itself was discouraged outside of lessons.

That's not to say it didn't happen, especially when children leapt into the deep end.

It was a Saturday, which is only significant due to the number of small children that were in the pool celebrating a birthday. There was a lane sectioned off for serious swimmers, who weren't put off by the noise and flurry of activity that 8- and 9-year-olds are prone to, so they could swim lengths unimpeded. One elderly woman, called Barbara Scale who was retired and volunteered at a local wildlife sanctuary, kept her swim-capped head above water as she gracefully breast-stroked her way from one end of the pool to the other, and Nathan Rigge, a middle-aged man, who I have since learnt was going through something of a midlife crisis health kick. He wore a smartwatch that timed his heart rate, laps, and oxygen consumption. His wife later told me that he wasn't an expert, and refused to speak with an expert, but would read up on online message boards how to improve his stroke. He spent several hours that morning lapping Barbara Scale with a chaotic version of front crawl. They were the only people sharing that lane that morning.

The birthday party was that of 9-year old Tom Hebblethwaite, who lived less than a stone's throw away from the pool and had invited ten of his best friends ([1] Noah Taylor, Oliver Heap, George Arrowsmith, Leo Blevin, Oscar Standish, twins Roman and Isla Calderbank, and Toby and Scarlett Wright (unrelated) – all aged between 8 and 9.) to join him at the pool. His mother, Della, was watching from the side of the pool and his father, John, watched from behind the glass in the waiting area. John was not a strong swimmer and a little embarrassed to be in the pool. He brought a book to read, but smiled at the sight of his son, daughter, and their friends swimming so strongly.

All eleven party children were strong swimmers as all of them learnt to swim in lessons at the same pool, and many also swam as part of the club that ran practices daily. Mrs Idam, mother of Jolly Idam, was also there to make up numbers in the ratio of adults to children. Tom's younger sister, Jess, along with her friend, Kelly Holme, stayed in the shallow end, watched over by John Hebblewhite's mother, Nora. Nora was also not much of a swimmer, but had been brought up to be cautious of the water and was therefore happy to watch over the girls as long as she could stand in the water.

In the deep end, Max Nailor, Gavin Mercer and Rob Cook splashed two girls they knew from high school. The boys had wanted to go up to the quarry to swim, but had been driven to the pool when the weather turned. It is not clear if the two girls, Gina Catterall and Grace Hurstwood, had been invited by the boys to the quarry and ended up in the pool with them, or whether this had been a separate arrangement. The five of them played a little rowdily, testing strength and skill using the weights that the lifeguard, Helen Davie, had put out for the children's party, dropping them to the bottom of the pool and racing to pick them up, or seeing how long they could hold their breaths whilst sitting at the bottom of the pool.

The names of those present are only important in so far as they name those present in the pool that day. It might be crass to suggest that the names are not important as it implies the people were not important either. I battled myself the best way to present the names and the people in this report and came to the only conclusion possible. The names were needed.

It wasn't until 11:10 that any concerns were raised. The first sign that something was amiss was the children complaining of feeling tired and finding it difficult to swim. Della Hebblethwaite considered pulling the party from the water and moving on to the home disco and cake, but had spent so much on entrance fees for all of the children for an hour of swimming that she didn't.

Elsewhere in the pool, others were beginning to feel tired, their movements became sluggish and difficult. Even the stronger swimmers began to feel it. The last signal from Nathan Rigge's smart watch showed his lap time had slowed by 12 seconds. There were no further readings pinged to his phone.

Oliver Heap, the only child to survive unscathed, came out of the water due to an asthma attack. He sat with his back against the wall, water running off him as he struggled to breathe, whilst Della Hebblethwaite raced to get his inhaler from the locker room.

Oliver Heap watched everything from a state of emergency and panic. Due to his state at the time of the event, and trauma of what occurred, he was never called to provide testimony. It was decided that forcing the boy to relive and recount his experiences would add no tangible evidence and would do significantly more damage than good.

It was whilst Della's back was turned that the pool fell silent. It wasn't a hush that quickly dampened the noise, it was a sudden and audible break in the sound, as though someone had pushed mute by mistake. The splashing stopped mid-splash, the excited calls of the children's party were cut off and their echo suppressed. There was a scrape from the lifeguard's chair against the tiled surface, and then a shrill cry from little Jess Hebblethwaite.

Della turned to see the frozen tableau of the pool. For a moment it appeared to be a photograph of the day. Still water, still bodies in the water. But the lifeguard, Helen, was moving, and her husband, John, had stood up at the window that looked into the pool to see what was going on.

In the shallow end of the pool, Jess, Kelly and Nora were standing stock still; Nora tugging at the ledge trying to prise herself from the water, to lift herself onto the side.

Halfway down the pool, Della could see the children's legs in the air, competing in a handstand competition – their legs waggling at the ankle, except for Noah Taylor who had been the judge, and Toby and Scarlett Wright who were the first to give up and return to the surface.

At the deep end, only Gina Catterall was visible, as she was trapped breaking the rules as she bombed into the pool, her knees and chest above the waterline, the rest of her submerged. The teens beneath her were all frozen underwater.

In the lane that ran alongside, Barbara Scale had just reached the shallow end and was about to turn. Her head remained above water but she was unable to turn her head and see what was happening in the rest of the pool. Nathan Rigge was caught mid-stroke coming up for air. His face turned to the side waiting to break the surface. Both Della and Helen claimed to see his eyes move in his goggles for almost a minute after the water stopped.

John Hebblethwaite ran through the changing rooms onto the pool side to try and help his mother and daughter out of the pool. Helen Davie tried to use her bodyweight to break into the water to help, but only managed to fracture her ankle and live thereafter with a limp.

The handstand competitors' feet stopped twitching. Noah Taylor, Toby and Scarlett Wright, began crying, complaining that it hurt. As did Jess and her friend Kelly. Nora told her son that the water round her legs was getting tighter, and she could no longer feel her toes. Della tried to pull Jess from the water, fearful that the water was somehow suffocating her as she stood chest high in it. But the only body part above water was the child's head, and she screamed as her mother pulled her hair and ears trying to release her from the grip.

The alarm was raised by John, whose phone was thankfully in his trouser pocket and not the jacket that he had left in the waiting room. He called 999, and when asked what he needed he demanded they send everything.

The firefighters arrived first. They came in to inspect the situation, only knowing that there wasn't a fire. Many of them were too shocked to do anything useful. A fire was one thing. A fire was a situation that was practised. Battling flames and chaos was something that they became accustomed to over time, but the Cragforth pool incident challenged the fabric of their reality. Water was their weapon of choice, and water was no longer safe.

The builders on a local construction site along with some road workers on a project on the motorway close by were called down to the pool, along with their power tools. The theory put forward by some first responders was that they could perhaps dig out the living children. There wasn't time for an assessment beyond the desperation of the event. They brought pneumatic drills, pickaxes and sledgehammers. But all the tools glanced off the water, and made no dent or impression at all on the solid ripples.

Lonnie Jump, the foreman on the construction site, had the idea to use crowbars and slide them down the gap where the water met the wall of the pool, but there either was no gap (and the water was anchored onto the wall itself) or the gap was too slight and impossible to fit anything of substance down.

Soon, it seemed the whole town had made its way to the pool. They gathered on the football pitch that backed onto the pool's building. Fascinated, but fearful of getting too close to the water and being swallowed themselves, but too emotional and curious to stay away.

Jess Hebblethwaite and her friend Kelly Holme only survived an hour or so before their lungs were crushed by the weight of the water that refused to let them go. Kelly Holmes' parents arrived too late to say goodbye to their beloved daughter, but Kelly was held and loved by Della and Nora in her final moments, which did give Mr and Mrs Holmes some comfort.

The three children in the party in the mid-section of the pool whose heads were above water, lasted between 4 and 26 hours. Their ribs were a little stronger and they held on much longer than the smaller girls.

I don't wish to go into the final agonising hours of those trapped with their heads above water. The medical report filed by the coroner goes into detail. They were children. Children surrounded by death scattered through solid water. In their last moments, they found it difficult and painful to breathe.

Barbara Scale outlived the children but died shortly after, from the same, crushing death. She spoke with her daughter on the phone as she passed.

Nora suffered a heart attack late on the first day. She had previously had heart problems, though the situation certainly had an effect on her physically and was listed as contributory to her cause of death.

Mrs Idam, who held her infant son aloft for nearly three days, finally succumbed to her fate. A nurse took over holding Jolly, and a team of surgeons came in – there is no delicate way of saying this – to separate the parts of Jolly that were encased in the water from the rest of his body in order to remove him from the pool before it took his life. The boy lost most of his left leg, and his right foot. I have heard since that he recovered and is doing quite well in physical therapy.

The last to go was Gina Catterall. From her position, half in and half out of the water at the deep end facing down the full length of the pool, she could see all the suspended bodies, and the left behind limbs of poor Jolly Idam. She could turn nowhere; she could avoid none of it. It's difficult to know her cause of death for certain, but from the descriptions of her pain that she gave the doctor and her parents who stayed with her to the end, the cause was likely a ruptured bladder, unable to relieve itself, and the subsequent infection. At least, this was what was named on the death certificate.

The pool was closed off the day after Gina Catterall passed. The doors and windows blocked up with wooden boards on the inside and bricked up from the outside, to protect the final resting place; not that anyone ever went near the place. Even those in search of morbid thrills gave the pool a wide berth.

AUTHOR REDACTED

The town held a memorial to those who died, but there were no burials. The water kept the bodies.

LONG WAKE : COFFEE BREAK

The coffee machine in the hallway between reception and the outpatient clinic rejects his dollar bill once again, spitting it out with an aggressive tone. Adam takes the note and pulls it taught, trying to pull the creases out of it. He bends the bill over in his hand, trying to combat the deeper folds. He feeds the bill back into the machine and prays that it takes it this time so that he can get his caffeine fix.

The coffee is awful. Powdered coffee and dried milk are dumped into the cup before it is slowly filled up with lukewarm water. The result is watery, burnt with a gritty aftertaste that coats his tongue in a thick slime.

Adam has been drinking this coffee for almost a month, making daily trips down to the machine and wasting away ten minutes stretching his legs before returning to his vigil at his wife's bedside.

The hospital never stops. Bustling and full of life. He knows there are many deaths there each day, he's seen the doctors and nurses weep in the privacy of their *staff only* rooms. He has become such a fixture that they no longer close the door on him.

Adam sips from his cup and passes an orderly who gives Adam a knowing look. Adam has yet to decipher their exact meanings. The whole gauntlet of political persuasion runs through the hospital and it's not always easy to tell who is sympathetic and who is truly sympathetic. If he knew; he would probably kill them. He was not an angry man, or a violent one, but even the pacifist can find his limits.

His office is understanding, thankfully, but he isn't sure how long their patience will last. They are giving him a wide berth, part of which, he suspects, is probably so they don't have to deal with any of the fallout, whatever way this goes. Insurance-wise, he doesn't have a clue. It makes no difference to him. He has no choice.

He downs his cup, and finds a new bill to pour a second which he carries back up to the room with him, taking the scenic route up a windowless staircase in the centre of the hospital, rather than the direct elevator.

Her room is always full of sound. He is used to watching her sleep and hearing only her gentle snores occasionally rising to a crescendo and a small cough before she would turn over and fall back into a heavy sleep. She had always been very conscious of her snores; afraid she would wake him. She did. Often. Not that he ever told her.

He misses the snores. He misses the bedding shift when she turned over and pulled the duvet with her. Then, when all the warmth had gone, she would turn back into him and nestle her head under his chin.

She was loud then, and the room is loud now. The constant hum of machinery, and the bellows breathing into her. The staircase is often the one place he can get any peace.

He hovers at the doorway. If he stands at just the right angle, he can pretend that she is just asleep and he is just bringing her coffee. But that fantasy is broken the moment he crosses the threshold. Here she is, lying under bleached, white sheets. Her body assaulted by wires and tubes. The only movement, her belly rising and falling.

She's dead. She has been for a while. Adam knows that. The doctors know. Everyone knows. She's dead. A corpse lies in that bed. A corpse he is not allowed to bury. The child in her womb kept going by the machines. His poor, unformed child that will *fail to thrive* outside.

Adam sits in the chair to continue his vigil and checks his phone. No news from the in-laws and their conversation with the lawyer. He isn't sure that *desecration* would mean that much to the powers that be who forced this situation.

Outside the window, down by the ambulance bay, were dozens of protestors, fractioned off into opposing parties. Preachers insisting on keeping an eye on the hospital to ensure that their law is followed to the letter, raising their voices to the heavens to keep their flock tight. Protestors shaking their fists at the injustice, others using the rallying point to shake their fists at all injustice.

Of all of them, it's the men and women silently holding the candlelight vigil that Adam hates the most. He can hear the preachers during the day, but they aren't allowed to raise their voice or gather at night. The vigil is silent. He often forgets they are there until he walks over to the window and sees their candles. A nurse informed him they whisper prayers. Prayers for the unborn child. Prayers for a miracle. Prayers He rejects.

They know his face now, the protestors. Someone broke in and got a photo of him by the bed and spread it on social media. It got to the point that every time he came and went, there would be people following him in, badgering him, condemning him, demanding answers, and worst of all, praising him. That bitter praise, as though there were something else that could be done. As though this were a choice he'd made.

Since his face was revealed, Adam hasn't left the hospital. He can't bear it. Hospital policy was broken. But it already had been to bend to the will of the law.

The administrator arranged a bed for him, but with restrictions and capacity of the hospital, the only space available was her room. His cot was set up at the foot of her bed. He can't sleep in the room with her corpse, so he doesn't often sleep.

At midnight through to the early hours, he would take a

walk around the hospital and swing by the maternity wing. A punishment. Self-flagellation. He listens to those in their labour, coached by midwives and doulas, with their partners standing by trying to help. He is reminded of a future that no longer exists.

From one of the small private rooms, kept separate for those who can't afford a private room, but due to circumstance require one, comes a girl with a protruding stomach, the unmistakable sign. She could hardly be a teenager.

He doesn't make eye contact with the girl, her angry father who calls her back into the room.

His mind remains blank. He has learnt how to not think. How to leave opinions formless. But every-so-often that training fails him. He makes his way back to the end of the corridor and back into the cooped-up room, noticing the flickering flames for the vigil below. He turns his back on them and looks at his wife.

She wanted a baby. She wanted to live. When those two statements are incompatible and the first is certain to die, the second statement is surely certain. Or, at least, Adam had always presumed so. He never thought this would, or even could, be the outcome. He hadn't been paying attention.

He wanted a baby too. This was all his doing.

Guilt gnaws his insides.

He returns to his chair to continue the long wake.

QUEUE HERE, PLEASE

There had always been a queue. Of that, if nothing else, Bea was sure. She had no memory of a time before the queue, and could not describe anything but the walls, floors and ceilings that had made up existence so far. Even in those brief moments that the queue went outdoors, Bea was conscious of its restrictions. She couldn't leave the queue; nor could she skip it. She could only wait, patiently or not, for the queue to move forward.

The queue did move, though often in odd and jarring ways. There would be sudden bursts of energy in which the people would suddenly dash forward only to come to a sudden and abrupt halt. For the most part, those queueing spent their time meandering forward in short shuffles, waiting for something exciting to happen. Fully aware that it seldom would.

The queue snaked round the waterfront near the city centre, and whilst Bea could see neither the front nor the back of the queue, she surmised that she was about halfway through it. There were the occasional signposts with large placards giving instructions. Bea often didn't bother reading them. They only said the same sort of thing; everything's fine: stay in the queue. Not that Bea, or indeed anyone around her, had ever left the queue.

It bothered her that she knew exactly what was waiting for her at the front of the queue, but anytime that she tried to discuss it with anyone, her neighbours would shush her. It wasn't dignified to ask. It wasn't her right to know. Bea suspected that none of them knew either, and her constant reminding irritated them. There would be a choice of doors at the front. There would be a puzzle. Complete the puzzle and a door would open and she would join the back of a new queue. What more could she need to know?

Bea counted her lucky stars that at this point in the queue, she had a good friend, Elle, who could take her mind off the unending queue. Bea did the same for Elle, and the two of them spent their time talking about something and nothing.

This isn't important. Or rather, it's only important in that they spoke and they got along. The details of their conversations are not important. Their conversations were to pass time as they shuffled forward.

Bea and Elle met a few doors ago. Their parents had disappeared a door or two earlier and hadn't reappeared. This wasn't uncommon, but it was distressing nonetheless. Elle had cried that whole first queue, and when Bea met her, her eyes were red raw. Bea couldn't remember what she had said to cheer Elle up, but she remembered Elle's chuckle, and their relationship grew from there.

There was a flurry of gossip running down the ground towards them. The doors had been spotted. The puzzle was known.

Two large, oak doors in front of which were a basket filled with coloured, plastic balls and a second basket to place the balls.

That was it. No instructions. No details. Nothing about what the balls meant or signified. The adults around Bea and Elle discussed intently what the balls could mean, what the colours could mean.

"What do you think?" Elle asked, peering round the hips of the woman in front of her.

Bea shrugged. "You look to see what the queue looks when they go through that door and I'll look at what it looks like through this door."

The queue was moving forward, but even as the girls got closer, they couldn't see the next queues through the doors.

When it came to their turn, Elle went first. "Red," she said, picking up a shiny red ball and dropping it into the basket. The door to the left opened and she went through.

"Red," said Bea, mimicking the exact movements Elle made and dropped the ball into the basket. The door to the left opened and she went through.

"Are there ever seats?" Bea asked, her legs aching, as she looked round the grimy corridor they were in. The ceiling was low, the walls stifling close together, almost pressing in on them, and they were damp and dank to the touch. It smelled strongly of body odour and decomposing waste. There were no recesses, no doors, nothing but a straight corridor that felt as though they were climbing upwards, with flickering lights and cobwebs where the walls met the ceiling.

"I'm sure I've been somewhere with seats," Bea went on. "But maybe it was a long time ago."

Elle smiled and said nothing, simply relieved that Bea had made it through to the same queue and the two of them were together again.

The teenage boy in front of them piped up. "It's awful not having anywhere to sit. I've always had somewhere to sit. It's terrible that we have to suffer here like this."

"It's not that bad," said Elle.

"Not that bad!" Jay scoffed.

"I've been worse," she clarified.

"God!" he exclaimed and turned to face the front of the queue.

Elle began to fidget. Her whole body twisted and strained. She whispered in Bea's ear. "I really need the toilet."

Bea looked around but couldn't see any sign for toilets, or any indication that there would be space later.

"Just go against the wall," Jay said, still listening into their conversation. "You won't exactly lower the standards of the place."

Jay was right, to some extent, but Elle couldn't bear the thought of embarrassing herself in public.

Bea reached over Jay and tapped the woman in front of him on the shoulder. "Excuse me, do you know if there are any toilets?"

The woman shook her head and shrugged. "Not that I've seen," she said. "There's a woman a bit in front of me who's got one of them funnels. I can ask her for it, if you like?"

Bea didn't have to wait for an answer from Elle, who looked disgusted at the thought of sharing. "No, thanks. Thank you." Bea waved as she disappeared behind Jay.

Elle's face began to crumple. Her bottom lip trembled and she bit her lips between her teeth, scrunching her eyes shut in hopes that that would dull the motion. But she couldn't help it. The tops of her thighs rubbed together as she tried to dance the sensation away. "Bea!" She implored.

"Look," said Bea. "You have to go. I'll stand here so no one can see you, ok?"

Elle shamefaced and tearful, squatted on the ground to relieve herself. Bea could hear the quiet sobs of humiliation as the long, forceful stream could be heard.

Jay watched. His nose crunched into his forehead, but he didn't turn away. He didn't give her any privacy.

Ella stood back up and leant against the opposite wall. Tears ran down her face as she choked back a cry.

The odour was strong, not particularly different from the rest of the corridor, but fresher and more concentrated. Bea took Ella's hand and the two of them stood quietly for a moment.

"Eugh!" An old man behind them bellowed. "Who did that? Who is the dirty fucker that did that?"

Elle's face burned red. She tried to turn to look at the man, but Bea held her hand tight and refused to let her turn. Bea looked at the man as he hopped from one foot to the other. "Come on! Own up! Who's the dirty pisser?"

Bea looked down and saw how the urine was running down the queue. How the floor tilted slightly.

"It must be one of you lot," a woman behind the old man shouted. "Who was it?"

"That prick," the old man jutted a manicured finger at Jay. "I bet it was him."

"It wasn't me," Jay said, disgusted at the accusation. Bea looked up at him imploringly. Jay sneered "It was her," he said, pointing at Elle. "I saw her."

Elle covered her face with trembling hands. She wept into Bea's shoulder.

"She was desperate," Bea shouted as the rest of the queue started baying. "She was just desperate."

"Look at my shoes!" the old man shouted, lifting his feet up to show the wet soles. "Just look at my shoes!"

The yelling grew as the wee reached further and further back in the queue. Elle wanted the ground to swallow her whole and let her die. But Bea kept shouting back at them, cursing them at the top of her lungs, and came two steps to slapping Jay for egging them on.

Jay laughed once more, and decided he was done. He jumped the queue and reached the door, placing his thumb on a pad which opened a door to the right with a mahogany staircase going up.

The jeering petered out after that, and was replaced with bitter and angry whispers. 'How dare he skip the queue', 'who does he think he is?'. Bea was just glad that the attention was away from them. By the time they reached the front of the queue, no one was shouting at them anymore. Apart from the disgusted looks that were thrown Elle's way, no one spoke to them.

Bea looked at the puzzle by the door. A single stemmed abacus with a dozen stones on it, hanging horizontally on the wall. No instructions. No indication of what to do. Bea wasn't sure what it meant, how to solve it, or whether there was even an answer to it. Behind her back, Elle held up her fingers to indicate to Bea what she intended to do. Six stones on one side, six on the other. Keep it simple. Keep it balanced. Hope for the best.

Bea copied her, stepped through the door and saw a different girl in front of her. Bea looked round, thinking that perhaps two queues were merging and that this girl was just between the two of them. She wondered how long it had been between Elle going through and Bea following. Seconds. It could only have been seconds.

Another person joined the queue behind Bea, and then another. Realisation crept over Bea as she grasped that Elle was not in front of her and was not coming through that door. Bea was on her own, and so was Elle.

The corridor wasn't terrible. It was lonely, but not terrible. There were occasionally plastic chairs that folded down from the walls and provided an uncomfortable relief, but without Elle, Bea shifted uncomfortably. The last time they were separated was many doors ago. When they were reunited, Elle was quieter, smaller and more still than before. Elle never said what happened in their brief time apart.

"Hello," Bea says to the teenage girl in front of her. The teen doesn't turn around. Doesn't even acknowledge her existence. Bea turns to the woman behind and smiles. "Hi." The woman behind her says nothing either. Bea turns back to face the front and shifts uneasily until the queue finally takes a single step forward. Then the tension builds in her legs again, and she rocks from side to side, unable to let go of the unease.

Bea can't see the next door. This happened sometimes. Queues could be insanely long, they could twist so far to one side that not only could you not see the door, you couldn't even see the curve.

There was a small draft coming from the front of the queue. Bea could make out a light, but it wasn't until she got closer that she could hear people in a large open hall. She stepped out of the corridor and into a hall the size of a school gym. Shiny wooden floors and high vaulted ceiling. People were still lined up. Five or six feet separated Bea from the queues either side of her.

Bea wasn't the only person looking round in astonishment. After so many years being cramped in various queues, the sudden vastness intimidated her. She felt exposed. It was bright and airy. Very few people spoke. Even though she couldn't see any barriers, Bea was acutely aware that she couldn't leave her line. An imperceptible barrier between them.

Bea stood on her toes to see as far as she could. Others were doing the same. She saw a hand waving four of five queues away. It was Elle, standing en pointe, stretching up as far up as she could, waving manically.

Bea smiled broadly. She waved so enthusiastically that she almost knocked into the woman in front of her. She wanted to cross the room, to sweep her arms round Elle and hold onto her as tightly as she could, but she couldn't. She couldn't leave her queue. Even with no one watching. Even without the walls separating them, Bea was compelled to stay in her lane.

Elle reached the doors first. Waving goodbye to Bea, she picked up a block and turned it over in her hand. Bea looked at the one the woman in front of her was looking at, but kept jutting her eyes back to Elle to see what she was doing, making sure she didn't miss Elle's answer. The block was about two inches long, uneven in length, and cylindrical. In front of her were four holes. A circle, a rectangle, a triangle and a square the size of a fist. Bea realised that the block could fit snugly into any of the first three or be simply dropped into the last hole. She watched Elle choose the circle and step through the door.

Bea waited for the woman in front of her to shrug and drop the shape into the large square and walk through the door, before taking a step forward, picking up a block herself and pushing it through the circle.

The door didn't open. She looked around for assistance, but before she could even call out, the ground beneath her opened and she fell through a trap door into a snow drift.

Bea's breath came out in short puffs of cloud, hanging frozen in the air around her. The cold hit her lungs like sharp needles stabbing the inside of her chest. She covered her mouth, trying to warm the air before it got to her mouth. Then firmly rubbed her exposed arms, desperately massaging warmth back into them.

Her knees were frozen stiff, bruised from the fall. They ached as she clambered to her feet, brushing the frost from her trousers. The air bit, sinking its icy teeth into her skin.

She looked around.

No queue.

No other people at all.

Bea couldn't remember it ever being so quiet. So empty. She could see a dozen miles in any direction, the vastness was overwhelming. Daunting, even. It was physically painful to have the entire horizon, the entire 360-degree horizon, vast and endless and frozen.

Fear or the sudden cold; she began to cry.

Bea walked down towards a patch of trees, hoping, naively, that they would provide some warmth, or at least some cover from the bitter wind. Tear-filled eyes, burning freeze, blurring her sight, crusting her eyelashes shut.

"Hello?" Bea cried out, but her words were lost on the wind, whipped back over her shoulder. Wrapping her arms round her stomach and clutching tight, holding onto the last remnants of warmth. "Hello?" she cried louder and louder until her voice, hoarse with effort, gave out.

She stumbled through the wooded area. There was no door, no way out, no directions, no sign of life. She was lost. She trudged on voiceless through the barren landscape, then began to cry out when she thought she saw people in the distance. People, it turned out, that were just oddly shaped trees.

A scream shot down Bea's ears, and struck her ear drum with a pin. She spun round to try and pinpoint the origin of the piercing sound that kept ringing in her ears. The frozen land was still, but in the distance, so far away that Bea could only make out a blur lumbering between the trees, something moved.

Bea hid behind a tree, squashing her back into the trunk so hard that she could feel the rough bark scrape her shoulders as she breathed in. She covered her mouth with her hands, desperate to hold in the frozen smoke she breathed out. Desperate not to grow colder as she stood still.

Bea could hear the shadowy figure slowly walk. She could hear it sniff and pant. It was so close, she could feel it inside her head. She shivered violently. The fine hairs on her arm stood on end, as her skin puckered up. She desperately searched for somewhere to run to; anywhere that would be safe.

The low sun threw a dazzling sunset across the landscape and caught the corner of a door that suddenly appeared, standing between the trees. Bea drew deep breaths, freezing her lungs and stomach, readying herself to run. The heels of her feet pushed against the roots that rose from the frozen earth; she hoped that this would give her a split-second advantage.

She sprinted, heart pounding, lungs burning. Her feet slipping and stumbling over the roots that crossed her path. Arm reaching out to the door, fingers stretching out ready to grasp it.

The shadow screaming like a banshee now focused on her. Its thundering feet galloping towards her, striking the earth like a drum. The sound echoed through Bea's feet as they struck the ground.

She ran faster than she had ever before. She grasped hold of the door handle and pulled with all her might... but the door didn't move. The wood stuck, frozen to its frame. She beat the doors with her small fists, rattling it and tugging with all her might, desperately heaving the door towards her. But it was shut fast; welded to the spot. Bea cried out, hearing the running thud of the shadow. The deep roaring yowl and the ear-splitting screech as it closed the gap between them. Bea pulled with all her might, shoving the door, pushing it, pulling it, but it didn't move. Tears stream down her face as she screams, kicking, begging at the top of her lungs and scratching at the wood with bloody fingers.

ROOK AT LOVELL BANK

Not knowing what I was doing, and in fear of making things worse, I abandoned my attempt to fix the engine and dropped down the car bonnet to cover it from the elements. I hadn't much of an inkling where I was and could see no further than the end of my outstretched arm. The road disappeared quickly in both directions and I was dimly aware of a sudden drop onto the moor to my left, though I couldn't see it myself.

Getting back into the car, I pulled a map out of the glove compartment and checked the radio's clock. I had passed a village some twenty minutes ago and hadn't been travelling fast. The single road that crossed the moor was narrow and curved but didn't branch. I hadn't seen signposts for the next village so I probably wasn't closer to that.

I appeared to be between the two small villages of Rawstock and Leklem. I couldn't tell which I was closer to and either was too much of a walk in those terrible conditions. I resigned myself to staying overnight in my vehicle and tried to hunker down for warmth – though this was impossible as any warmth that had been spluttered from my heating before I stalled had been leached from the car and I was left miserably cold.

Still reading my map, as I had nothing else to entertain myself, I found a peculiar symbol that couldn't have been more than a mile from where I was sitting. Unfamiliar with the symbol, I turned to the key to find that it had been torn off by the previous owner. Using my lighter to fend off the growing darkness, I inspected the area more carefully. Whatever the mark represented appeared to be in the centre of a smattering of buildings labelled Lovell Bank, though what those were I couldn't tell.

Hoping to find farm buildings and sure I wouldn't be turned away at this time on such a dismal evening, I set off in a small break in the weather to find this set of buildings. Within a half hour I found evidence of a small, track road like you might find on a farm with two deep trenches made by worn tyres. These had quickly filled with water, but I followed them up to a wooden hut.

I knocked at the door of each building in turn and shouted through the cracks to be heard over the howling wind. Stumbling between the buildings blindly and tripping over a mound of freshly turned earth, I ended up face down in the mud.

A door swung open and a light gleamed upon me through the haze. Although obscured by the dense fog I saw a person standing there whose very presence struck fear into me. *Perhaps I have made a mistake,* I thought as I looked up at the imposing figure. Their wide-eyed panic stared down at me and I suspected it mirrored my own expression. All the colour had drained from their face. Perhaps I wouldn't be welcomed as I hoped I'd be.

"Good evening," I said, as is only polite and hoping that my cordial demeanour would allow me some hospitality on the part of my potential host.

On hearing my voice, the figure relaxed somewhat and, I thought, breathed a sigh of relief. They didn't move. They stood towering over me as I tried to extract myself from the dirt. Upon standing, I realised they were not, in fact, a giant, but indeed fairly average in height. We regarded one another for a moment. Then, finally, they stood back and I was given my invitation to enter.

I hadn't been able to see the scale of the building, but once inside I was confronted with its immediate grandeur. A huge domed observatory and, at the very centre of the room, a telescope that filled the height of the building. The room was grand, though very much a working space. Rather than the ornate details of an expensive toy, the room had coarse iron finishings and each inch of space was crowded with papers and scientific instruments that I did not recognise and could not imagine their use.

The person returned and handed me a towel and some dry clothing. It was then I realised I was shivering from the cold. They motioned to a door to my left where I dried and changed myself in a small utility cupboard. The shirt and trousers I had been given were a little large, and I was grateful my host had seemingly already taken this into account and had given me a belt as well. The clothes had been recently cleaned – though I noticed the faint scent of another on the jumper as I pulled it over my head.

It must be noted at this point that I don't entirely trust my own opinion. I can't count the number of times I have been led astray by this person or that down a warren of lies and trouble. I have good friends that I usually seek advice from before befriending anyone new. Each of those friends has earned my trust over years of steadfast assistance and my parents' approval.

I daren't think where or what I would be without them.

So, there I was, unable to obtain the reliable opinion of a trusted ally. When I re-entered the room to find my host, whom I suspected was an astronomer, physicist or perhaps engineer – I couldn't tell, and to this day I am unsure – sitting with their back to me. I decided to embrace caution and have as little interaction with them as possible and hoping that the morning would come soon and I would be able to return to my car.

Not wanting to appear rude though, I introduced myself but received no response.

"Do you have the time?" I asked, hoping that a direct question would elicit some form of response.

The physicist turned to me, seemingly surprised by my question. They looked up at a large clock that hung from the balcony. "A little after four," they said, and I felt the shame of embarrassment run down my face for having disturbed them. They returned to their books.

I took a turn around the room, careful to keep the scientist in view at all times. Their silent movements somehow made quieter by the wind whipping round the building. A fervent pen flicked across the paper and left a trail of ink but not a single scratch. Crumpled, raven hair falling into their eyes. Their light shirt lined with lace open to the sternum and trousers with braces hanging loosely by their legs, a state of undress that I was more than a little surprised by. Looking around the room I comforted myself that this was perhaps due to the observatory functioning as a lab, office and home and presuming they would have no guests this evening they had dressed hastily when hearing me stumble about outside.

There was, barely visible at their wrist, a smudge of dried mud. I must have brushed past them too closely as apart from this speck, they appeared meticulously clean.

I looked for somewhere to sit, as my put-upon host had not offered one. There were surprisingly limited options in the room. The physicist had the most prominent chair that they were sitting in with legs tucked beneath them but my vantage point they were sitting in such a peculiar way that they appeared to be floating above the chair.

I thought I might have to sit on a step or perhaps in the reclining seat of the telescope, but upon reaching the far side of the room I could finally see a chair at a second desk, again covered in so many papers, some of which had fallen on the floor. A cold mug of tea sitting on a stack it had spilt on. I picked it up and tried to wipe off the tea before it stained and ruined the work. I sat myself in the old office chair and spun myself a little so I could still see the physicist. I began tapping the armrests with my fingers. I was aware they were watching me out of the corner of their eye, and were not, in fact, reading.

"Do you have a partner?" I asked and saw their hackles flare up. "Colleague?" I corrected myself.

"Yes," the resigned answer came. "I do," they added carefully.

"Are they around?"

The physicist didn't right away answer, and instead busied themselves in a series of equations. "They took the car and left for town the day before yesterday. When they heard the weather was going to change. There is not much point of us both being here." Although they spoke with a dismissive tone, each considered word was clipped carefully.

"What kind of work do you do here?" I asked, again forgetting I was to keep myself to myself.

"I look at the universe," they said and nothing more.

"Not much to see tonight," I said.

"No, not much," they agreed, picking up a box of tools and searching through it until they found a wrench they were looking for. There was a break in my host's movements, a tightening of the brow as though considering a chess match. "Are you any good at holding a rope steady?"

"Er, yes," I said, caught off guard. "I can do that."

They handed me an end of rope and clipped themselves into a harness. "Don't let go," they said and pulled down a lever attached to a wheel of wound-up rope. The physicist flew up into the air and a heavy sack thudded into the floor spilling fine powder on the floor. I soon discovered it was my job to use the guide rope to direct my flying host round the telescope so they might make repairs.

The genius of the mechanism was not lost on me, though I admit I could not follow the logic of it. The graceful movements of the figure above made me appreciate the delicate balance and fight against gravity. I suspected the rope in my hands was new as it appeared unused, but found a short stick of something stabbing at my palm. I carefully orientated the rope in such a way that I could pick out the splinter without letting go of the rope. I found a shard of fingernail, though I could not tell if it had come from myself or my host or even their colleague. I tried to pick it out, but was unable to.

I had anticipated that the scientist flying above me would have been delicate and precise in their movements, but was surprised to find them quite clumsy, not ungraceful but perhaps 'cloddish'. They moved deftly, but dropped tools that came clashing to the ground and making a mess around the place.

"Let me down slowly," they said. They removed their harness and thanked me. The gratitude came as a surprise and was the first nicety that my host had given. "I'm sorry, I don't know your name?" I gave it gladly and asked for theirs in return. They repeated their thanks to me, taking care to address me by my full name, which I thought kind, before saying "Rook," but made no indication as to whether it was a first or surname, or simply the name they were known by. Their lips turned up into a grateful smile, a thinking-person's smile, one that I had seen on my professors when I tried to answer questions in class and usually got the answers spectacularly wrong.

I smiled in return.

"Oh dear," I exclaimed as I went back to my seat and noticed the trail of mud I had dragged round the room with me. "Oh, I am terribly sorry!" I begged forgiveness and access to a mop and bucket. But Rook smiled quite rakishly, entertained by me.

"Nevermind," they smirked and dismissed my offer of cleaning.

"No, but look here," I said. "I've managed to make such a terrible mess of things. There is mud everywhere, my grubby hands have touched nearly everything!"

"Nevermind." Rook's smile grew by inches and curved round their face to touch each ear, as though smiling at a joke I was not a party to.

It was now a moment to six by the clock on the balcony and by then the storm had calmed down. Upon opening the door, we found the fog had thinned into a dense mist; one I could see through and past the empty courtyard down the fresh track to the road below along which my car was abandoned. Rook gave me my clothes, which I now saw small tears in, which I must have acquired when falling and even a larger rip at the shoulder I had no memory of getting. My poor, distressed clothes, I accepted, may need to be thrown.

I pointed to the rise of turned earth I had tripped over several hours earlier, that I could now see was beside the observatory's car. The mound had sunk a little beneath the torrential rain, but was still holding its shape. Rook was still smiling and nodding to me. I set off to find my car and my way home.

DITCH

You should get up. Lying on your side like that is going to get uncomfortable soon. I'm sure you're already beginning to ache – that dull groan in your muscles is only going to get worse. The tear in your shirt at the button near the collar keeps pulling. If you listen carefully, you can hear the thread ripping along the seam. Your shoulder scrapes against the carpeted interior of the car boot you are in. Your head knocks against the edge of a box that rattles about, like there are large marbles rattling inside that are nudging the box around when the car turns sharply at a corner.

Raise an arm above your head. Or, at least, try to. As you twist your arm up and round your body, you feel a tug on your other wrist. Your hands are bound together. A skinny rope digging into your flesh at the wrist and ankles, holding you together.

How about slower, smaller and more concentrated movements. Gently tease the rope so that it moves enough to slide your hands free. Slip the rope back and forth, squirm a small amount of space to worm out of. Hands first.

Hands first. Then it's your blindfold. Then the ankles. Hands, eyes, feet. Hands, eyes, feet. After that, you just have to work out how to get out of the boot of a moving car. Simples.

First thing's first: focus on the ropes around your wrists. That's the first thing, that's number one. Without that, you can't do anything else.

But the rope isn't moving. It isn't slackening. Instead, the rope seems to be getting tighter. Chaffing your skin raw; red-hot like the playground torture game of burns your friends played on you. That sounds pretty bad, I know. It sounds like they were bullies and not friends.

This isn't the time to dissect that part of your life.

A deep breath in grows into a yawn that expands your lungs into your shattered ribs, a stabbing pain as the car bumps over a rocky road and pierces your insides. The bones shifted further out of place with every jolt, knocking the remaining wind from you.

The drive is long and rough. Tyres rumble over gravel, kicking the small stones up into the undercarriage, like a hailstorm from below. The rattling of the chassis, and the rumbling of the engine; the car sounds old. And knocked about. Even though the car is moving with some speed, each deft turn of the wheel is confident and sure, suggesting the driver has been down this route before.

How long have you been here? I couldn't say; you were passed out for a long time. You are certainly out of town now. Maybe an hour. Maybe longer. I don't know. Without light it's hard to judge the length of time. I'm not even sure how and where they found you. That knock on our head was pretty hard. Was there blood? You went down pretty hard. I don't remember any staggering about. Can you feel a damp patch in your hair? I can't tell from here.

The car pulls over. The engine chuggers and then stops. The driver's door clicks open and the weight of the driver exiting the car lifts the body of the car. The car lets out a groan and you are tipped, but roll back into place. The boot door clicks open and the faint light is enough to stab you through the eyes. A halo blazons round the head of the driver, blotting out his face with shadow. He pulls your body out of the boot and drags you over the rough ground to the verge, and with a swift kick to the torso, he sends your spiralling down a short hill into an overgrown ditch.

Open your eyes.

Light bleeds through the leaves and soft, wide-bladed grass. You are face down in the mud. It rained here not too long ago. As you breathe, the water at rest on top of the mud quivers. Your clothes draw in the water. The wet against your skin is so cold it sends a long shiver through your body. With great effort, you force your body to roll onto its back and watch the daylight fade away.

Close your eyes.

The car's engine sputters back to life and you hear as the tread grasps the road until it gets traction and drives away. A soft roar, the kicking of stones, and it slinks off into the distance, leaving you beneath a cold, indifferent sky.

Limbs groan as they twist and settle into their new resting space. Your muscles are tense. Trying, through sheer will, to hold you out of the wet mud, but failing. Your skin forms goosebumps that travel up your arms and legs and stands the hair on end. Your fingertips prune in the mud behind your back and grow immensely painful, until the cold takes away all feeling.

Night falls; moonless, starless. You fade into the inky black.

"I'm ok," you whisper to the universe, as if saying that would make it so. The universe, you and I all know you're lying, but we don't say anything. It's unfair to kick someone when they're down.

Your breathing slows. Shallows. Every muscle lets go and the gap between each heartbeat grows until the gap doesn't end and your heart stops.

Time falls in on itself and every past moment lives inside you in an instant. Your heart petrifies; the stone sinking to the back of your chest. Memories attack; the ones you don't want. Blending the undesirable together in a ball of painful feeling. All those things you try to forget. All that bitterness and spite and anger that burnt away inside you and you thought was forgotten, it all comes back in a heap. There are good memories. Somewhere. Probably. But you just can't quite remember where you put them.

You die.

Alone.

I heard once that we all die alone, but that's not quite true, is it? Death is a solitary act, to be sure, so even in the midst of war and pandemic, each death is a solo event experienced by one person. But it doesn't have to be lonely. You could be surrounded by loved ones in a comfortable bed, surrounded by the aroma of good food, and by music and art and love and joy.

But here you are.

You are here alone.

And you die here, alone.

Lying in the dirt. The weight of your body pulling you into the sodden earth. Night air cools your skin, leaching warmth and leaving your skin cold to the touch. The cold works its way to the core until there is no difference between your meat and that of surroundings.

I'm still here, watching you, being sucked ever deeper into the sludge.

'Am I dead?' You ask yourself. The question puzzles you, or rather, the act of asking yourself, especially as you most certainly are.

The living still make their noise above ground. The wind, rustling through the trees. A scavenger comes sniffling at the sole of your foot with a wet nose that runs a slick of mucus into the arch. Licking your ankle. Carefully, cautiously even, the fox sinks its teeth into your foot and grunts as it tugs your leg, jerking your whole body as its sharp teeth and claws tear at your calf and scrape along the shin bone until it tears the cartilage at the ankle and rips your foot off. The fox picks up its prize and trots off back to its den.

It'll be back for more of you.

Muscles stiffen into a rigid casket around your body. Stiffness of death. Rigor mortis. It's odd to feel this from the inside. But how many dead bodies do you even see these days? How many dead bodies do you even touch? The occasional open casket. An old man on the bus. A heart attack in town. But you're not supposed to touch. Never permitted to know. So, even though you can't move, your body tightens around your bones.

Flies find you next, searching out the early smell of death. They land on your skin – their six small feet tapping lighting as they travel along your arm, nudging past the fine hair and into the crook of the elbow. Another, lands on your eye – raising its front legs and slowly cleans its face and antennae, brushing miniscule debris away and catching the edge of your eyelashes with every stroke. Satisfied that it's now clean, the fly plods down into the corner of your eye and slips between the slit, burrowing down into the soft tissue of the eyes, ripping off small chunks of eyeball to make space in which to lay eggs. Tiny, gooey blobs begin to fill the eye socket. After laying its eggs, the fly, exhausted, crawls out and flies off.

More flies find what was your body. Making nests in the mouth, crawling up through the nose and down through the cavity to lay eggs in the soft palate at the top of the throat.

A slow, creeping centipede tracks up the inside of the thigh – each foot blending into one continuous pressure snaking over the skin. It's not here to eat you, it's just curious. A beetle flops heavily on the drum skin of your stomach, testing the skin by kneading it before nibbling away at the belly. A small swarm begins to nip away at the flesh and burrow into the intestines.

The sun rises, but doesn't warm. Flowerheads turn to soak in its warmth and bask in the weak glow.

Birds land and pick at your cheek – the plump flesh, though cold and lifeless, and growing ever tougher, is still so tempting.

Larger scavengers make off with your limbs, dragging hunks of you back to feed their young.

Rain drips. Slow drops at first, but then begins to flatten the grass and ferns around your body. Water pools on leaves and large droplets form and come crashing to the earth. Water runs over your skin and fills the pores and the cavity in the belly. You begin to fuse with the ground below.

Nestled safely in your eye, hidden from dangers of the outside world, the eggs crack and open. Tiny maggots begin to wriggle over one another in their first thirst for life, eating the rich pickings their good mother found for them. The eyeball, the muscle, through the soft palate and tongue, eating you from the inside out. Each maggot taking a small amount of you and growing, gaining. Once tiny maggots, eggs barely visible to the naked eye, have grown from tiny grains of rice to nice, fat grubs the size of grapes, a writhing pile of ravenous minibeasts outgrowing their birthplace. With so many insatiable mouths, you are soon nibbled down to the bone.

Your jaw falls open and the maggots spill out onto your neck and fall to the ground.

The larvae in your gut have also grown fat. They begin to march up your torso, both inside and out, making a final charge for what is left of your face. Everything exposed above the waterline is slowly taken away.

Your skin loosens and sloughs off – slipping down towards the earth. Blood sinks through your veins and pools into your back. Your skin sallows. Black blotches form around orifices, gases bloat your remaining organs – expanding and stretching what's left inside, until your guts break out. Liquid oozes from your skin and what has been green is now dying around you, poisoned by your death.

Leaves fall, burying you. Beetles and mites eat what remains of your hair, until your bones are exposed to the elements, and all the tiny creatures leave.

You are dispersed. Each part of you is consumed and removed – separated from your core. What's left sinks into the mud and is buried by the falling leaves. You no longer exist. No longer are you.

AUTHOR REDACTED

No longer 'are'.

ROADMAN

I

It was whilst Ready was sitting in the barber's chair, with the surgeon's fingers deep in the wide-open wound cutting a wedge in his side, that he was taken back to the first stabbing he had been witness to all those years ago as a small boy in his mother's council house. A large, white man pounded at the door until it broke down and then stormed through to the kitchen where the small boy and his mother were hiding. Ready's mother had stood between the man and her boy with her kitchen knife in hand and pushed the metal to the hilt through the man's soft underbelly when he charged her.

There had been many, many knife attacks in the years since, but that first one had left an indelible stain on his heart. When his heart had been pierced and replaced with surgical steel and synthetic valves that ran on a bioelectrical charge, the sensation remained. The fear and panic he had felt as a small boy was re-etched into his new heart. .

He wrapped his mechanical knuckle round the end of the chair arm as the surgeon investigated deeper into his torso.

"What were you hit with, fam?"

"Machete," Ready told the surgeon through a hitched breath as a nerve in the bloody mess was tapped.

"I thought they'd been banned?" Surge rarely took interest in the legality of things. "Wasn't there an amnesty at the high school?

Those boxes to drop them in?" He preferred to judge criminality case-by-case, and that gave Ready a steady stream of jobs and a place to get patched up.

"There are less about," Ready admitted through gritted teeth. "You can still get your hands on them if you know people."

"It's a miracle you haven't bled out," the surgeon said, soaking up the blood with an oily rag. Ready hadn't thought of his survival as a miracle. He wasn't entirely sure he had survived. His heart was pumping at its usual speed, but the blood loss was already taking its toll. Ready felt lightheaded, his arms felt distant, and his legs had barely managed to carry him this far. His conscious thought rose out of his body and hovered above him, though his feet were still tethered within him and his mind was unable to travel any further due to the pain.

"Is there any proper damage?" Ready asked.

The surgeon sighed and leant back in his chair to give him enough space to wipe his forehead with the back of his forearm.

"You're gonna need another kidney," Surge told him. "Sooner rather than later. Looks like the tip of the blade sliced through the surface but didn't nick anything. I've meshed it, but that won't last long." Surge placed his fingers into Ready's side, gently pulling the skin and trying to draw the wound back together. He leans back, again, to think. "I'm going to have to patch this."

"Skin?"

"I've not got any of that."

Deft-skin it was then. Ready's hands and arms were covered in the stuff, concealing the mechanics of his hand. A leathery excuse for skin. Every update was slightly softer, but was always visibly different. The pores too wide, the hair too glossy. Even after pigment was added, no artist could ever get it dark enough to match his skin. It tanned differently too, never catching enough sun. In summer, Ready's body became a patchwork of skins.

"Is it gonna take long?"

"How pretty do you want it?" Surge asked, fumbling about in a drawer of spare parts that once made up a person.

Ready shrugged, not because he didn't care, but because it didn't matter how much he cared. The surgeon was a good patcher, he had held Ready together longer than anyone thought possible. He would prefer that the Deft-skin was as passable as possible.

"You gonna tell me who did this?" Surge asked, pulling a portable x-ray machine out of a wardrobe. "I'm not the cops you know. I'm not one of those jackbots. I'm not going to tell anyone."

Ready shrugged again. He could hear his mother telling him to stop shrugging, but really it was his way of giving himself space to think. He would never report this to the police, he had a deep distrust of them, and if anyone found out that he had squealed, he would be hounded out. He didn't believe in the whole 'deal with it yourself' attitude that many of his old friends adhered to. Still, even if he didn't believe it, he didn't go against it. That's where the shrug came in, his way to avoid saying aloud what he thought. His way of avoiding further damage.

'Damage'. Not 'pain'.

That phrasing probably said more about him than he cared to admit.

He certainly didn't want to draw the attention of the jackbots. They would probably take him in rather than investigate. The few encounters he had suffered with the 'bots, the less inclined he was to call for help.

He would never call for help.

"You've had work done elsewhere?" Surge broke into his thoughts.

"Hmm?"

"Your spine."

"Ah," said Ready, who took a deep breath in. "Yeah, whilst you were away. Fell off a roof." He tried to play this off with a small chuckle.

The surgeon made a pointed look over his glasses at Ready, who looked away to avoid his gaze. Ready could already hear the surgeon's thoughts. Whilst Surge had no issues with biohacks and mods, loving to play about with them and explore his interest in biomedical procedures, he was in a minority on the estate. Ready had had to travel for the work.

"And your lung?" the surgeon asked, inspecting the screen closely. "Is that a BIMEC?"

"I didn't ask," Ready admitted.

The surgeon put the x-ray device away. "Those things are toxic," he said. "They leak. They leak everything, everywhere. They leak air into your chest cavity, and they leak oil into your bloodstream. Nasty stuff."

"I didn't really have a choice," Ready said.

"You *always* have a choice," the surgeon said.

Not when you're unconscious, Ready thought.

"I'll keep a lookout for something better," the surgeon said, pulling out the Deft-skin and pigments. "You'll feel it wheeze. Let me know when that happens."

Ready nodded. The surgeon repositioned Ready's arm so It crooked over his head and his hand rested on his opposite shoulder, so that he could see the whole wound and decide the amount of skin that was needed. Too much, and Ready would be left saggy, too little and it would rip the first time Ready stretched.

II

Ready walked home with a swagger. He hoped that he looked hard, rather than sore and tight. He pulled his hoodie up over his head, bracing against the chilly night air, and hoping that even if he did pass someone that was looking for him, they might not recognise him right away, and he might have that split-second advantage to get home.

The barbershop was on the far side of the estate to his mum's house. This late at night, and with half the street lights popped, he decided to walk the periphery, the A-road that ran between his estate and the leafy suburb to the west. The A-road was well lit and had a constant, though light, stream of traffic. At one point the road had been much busier, but the traffic from the estate had been cut off a few years ago, an act blamed on multiple traffic incidents. Incidents that were attributed to the estate traffic, and not the leafy suburb. The only entrance/exit to the estate now, was down by a row of corner shops that backed onto the high school.

The suburb had shot themselves in the foot there. Rather than driving the half mile through the estate to drop their precious children off at school in safety, they were forced to drive around the estate. In morning traffic, it could take as long as 50 minutes. Their children weren't permitted to walk themselves through the dangerous *hood*.

Jackbots didn't patrol the A-road. They had little reason to. It was well-lit and maintained by the council. There were cameras that looked over the walls to monitor those walking on Ready's side of the street. The cameras that viewed the only regularly cleaned and repaired part of the estate. The jackbots preferred the dark recesses in the estate, where they weren't watched, where there were spaces they could curl up into, disjointed and set to monitor, waiting for anything suspicious. Anyone suspicious. Anyone who fitted their data-set definition of suspicious.

But Ready didn't see any jackbots on his way home. He didn't see anybody. A few cars passed by, but that was all. He wasn't stopped and asked where he was coming from or where he was going.

The path into the estate goes through a low thoroughfare under a block of flats. He's trodden this path so many times that his feet take him home, and all he has to do is focus on the ever-shifting shadows formed by the flickering of a broken street lamp. He had to step around the mountain of cardboard and rubbish that the council had on their list to pick up. A list that always had important and urgent refuse pick-ups pop up and push the estate's needs further and further down the queue.

The light was on in his mother's kitchen. He let himself in as the latch wasn't on yet, and went through to see her resting at the kitchen table, landline in hand, food bubbling in a pot on the stove.

Ready turned the heat down.

"No," his mother, Joyce, said. "It needs the heat."

Ready turned it back up and sat at the table with her.

"Where've you been?" she asked, looking up at the clock on the wall.

"Went to see Surge," Ready told her. "Didn't realise the time."

His mother worried about him, he knew that, but the worry he saw was different somehow. More pronounced. She rarely let him see her concern, waiting until his back was turned and he would catch a glimpse of her pained expression in the mirror. But this was not hidden.

"What are you doing up so late?" He asked her.

"Kenroy's gone missing," Joyce told him. "Your auntie is beside herself. She's gone out looking for him. I've called the hospitals and the police to see if they have him, but no one's seen or heard from him." Kenroy, not yet fifteen. "I thought maybe you were with him, but you didn't answer your phone." No, Ready didn't have his phone anymore. "I was hoping the two of you were just hanging out somewhere." Kenroy, who had always followed Ready about when they were kids, was not in the habit of following him around these days. "We don't know where he is."

Ready could see his mother's eyes droop as her head rolled forward, then suddenly spring back and pop open.

"Go to bed, mum," Ready said. "I'll go find him."

"But if the phone…" Joyce protested.

"Take the phone with you." His mother was a heavy sleeper, but the phone would surely wake her. "You're just gonna fall asleep at the table if you don't go to bed."

Reluctantly, sluggishly, Joyce picked herself up from the table and went through to her bedroom.

Ready hadn't spoken to Kenroy in the last six months. They hadn't fallen out, but Ready suspected that Kenroy was running with his old friends again, and that wasn't something that Ready wanted to be a part of.

He didn't have much choice now.

III

There weren't many places that Ready hadn't been on the estate. Most of the families that lived there worked in one of the nearby factories, or down in the shops on the high street and the shopping centre a short bus ride away. Anyone within a decade either side of him he knew from school and youth clubs that sprung up and collapsed on a regular basis. He had been inside most of the houses and flats, and recognised nearly everyone by face and name.

There had been trouble on the estate, there was always going to be trouble, but apart from a few minor scrapes in his youth, Ready was able to keep out of it. He had spent most of his teenage years boxing, then moved onto mixed martial arts, and although he was no longer allowed to compete, his reputation went before him. His skills had made him a target for people wanting to prove themselves, to build street cred, but Ready was never fully beaten.

He did regret not being allowed to complete anymore. The money had been good. And even though he had a job down at the mechanics, and the work Surge put his way, it never came close to his glory years. For a while, he would just walk around the estate, patrolling, he felt. Keeping an eye on things. He missed the fighting days of yesteryear.

Yesteryear? It had been one year. It had barely been 12 months since his last fight.

Still, these things couldn't be helped. He had lost a leg in an accident and had needed a new one. He could no longer compete either way.

He'd managed to get a good leg. The compensation covered that but nothing else. Further medical procedures were done by Surge, except for the times when Surge had been away and Ready had needed to see another, less reputable doctor – one who wasn't willing or able to talk in depth about Ready's medical history.

Counting up his body parts, Ready suspected that he weighed more in metal than muscle. The thought stewed in his mind and burned up like acid. It was all him, metal and muscle alike; but that didn't mean he was entirely happy about the situation.

It made him a target, regardless of how much he tried to keep out of trouble. Just like when he was a kid throwing stones at passing jackbots, he was now getting stones thrown at him. Stones, hands, knives.

Ready walked alongside the row of corner shops and went round the back of them, where the bins were piled high with plastic bags that spilled out onto the unpaved car park. There was an underground passageway that led onto the next estate behind the bins. Few people used it. The estate to the east was in the next postcode and the passageway formed such a tight bottleneck that no one dared use it.

No one, that is, except Ready. No tunnel could bottleneck a single man.

He wasn't sure what it was that brought him over to the next estate. He was simply following his feet. Trusting their differing intuitions. Their intuitions that were, for once, in tune with each other and Ready followed them.

At the tunnel's exit, Ready became aware of the red light of a camera. He was certain the lens was pointing directly at his face. His hood was pulled down over his forehead, covering his face, but the urge to turn and check had to be resisted. The urge to pull his hood down further had to be resisted. Ready became increasingly conscious of the way he moved in case in made him seem suspicious,

Ready prided himself on his complete control. He was in awe of how he was able to regulate his instincts.

Pride goes before destruction.

He was too busy patting himself on the back when the jackbot approached him.

"Where are you going?" the speaker buried in the Deft-skin asked.

Ready had a moment of panic. But his heart remained steady and his lungs remained open. The stir in his legs to bolt was only in his birth leg, and the replaced spine dampened that. The only place his fight or flight instinct remained intact was in his head.

"Where are you going?" the tinny voice repeated.

"Just out for a walk," Ready said, not wanting to draw attention to his missing, teenage cousin, not wanting to get the involvement of jackboots when it was at all avoidable.

"At this time of night?" the voice asked, suspiciously. Ready didn't know the speakers could inflect suspicion. Maybe he had just dreamt it. The 'bot didn't move. It stood firmly waiting for an answer.

"I was working late; I only just got off. I wanted a walk. There's nothing wrong with that," Ready spoke with a metered patience that he had acquired over time. Short simple statements that the bot would be able to process. "There's no curfew, is there?"

The jackbot's head jerked to the side. Ready suspected this had been programmed to make the machine look as though it were contemplating an answer, or searching for a thought.

"No curfew," the jackbot confirmed. "Suspicious activity in this area."

There was *always* suspicious activity in this area. Everything that happened in this area was labelled "suspicious".

Ready didn't ask if he fit the description of somebody that was reported as acting suspiciously, they often agreed that he did. "Can I go?" He asked.

The 'bot turned its head to the side again, and whilst its eyes shifted away from Ready, Ready knew that this was only for show and that the machine was completely focused on him. The jackbot continued to stare for an uncomfortable length of time and Ready shifted his weight from the ache of standing in one stance for too long.

The jackbot's eyes and head righted immediately.

"Do not run," it instructed.

"I'm not... I was just..." Ready started.

"Do not run," the 'bot continued. "You do not have authority to leave."

"I wasn't going to..." but again Ready was cut off.

"You do not have authority to leave," the 'bot repeated, grabbing hold of Ready's left arm and yanking it hard upwards.

"Woah! Steady on!" Ready exclaimed as his natural arm was almost popped from the socket. "I wasn't leaving!"

But the jackbot had had enough. With one swift movement, Ready came crashing to the floor, landing on his newly repaired side. He hadn't time to think, and yet before the 'bot could make its next move to shift him onto his front, pinning him in place, he took a hold of the jackbot's wrist and crushed the weak metal plates.

Jackbots can't express pain, because they don't feel it. They don't feel any emotion. And yet, even knowing this, Ready would have sworn he saw a look of confusion. Of distress. A look that any man would recognise in a fight that their opponent, the initiate, thought would be over quickly. The jackbot had messed up.

Ready struck the bot with a fist, dazing the circuits, then kicked up sharply. The bot did not let go – could not let go. The arm was crimped closed over an electric nerve, and the fingers would not release. Rather than stand and retreat a couple of steps, a move that Ready expected and anticipated, the 'bot was unable to untangle itself from Ready's left arm.

Ready pushed the jackbot over. He sat astride the central column and rained down fully fisted blows on the 'bot. His chest wheezed and stuttled as he exerted himself. He felt dizzy again. His vision blurred and he felt the BIMEC in his chest sting. Ready battled to remain conscious. Fought every faint spell with a forced widening of his eyes.

Before the jackbot was able to computate recovery, Ready took the blade from his belt and jabbed it into the jackbot's side, cutting through the metal plates and motherboard. He was able to wriggle his arm free of the jackbot's grip and stand above the hunk of metal that lay repeating the last action it had ordered.

Ready lifted his good leg and stomped the 'bot through its central circuitry.

IV

"Ready?" his mother called through from the kitchen. "Ready, are you up?" He wanted to shout through that he wasn't. He wanted to lie on the sofa until it was night again. But he was awake now, and even though he hadn't opened his eyes, Ready could see how bright the room was. He rolled into the sofa and covered his face with his hood.

Joyce came through to the living room. "You're awake," she told him, tapping him on the shoulder with the phone. "Surge is on the phone for you. Make it quick, I don't want to miss a call from your auntie."

Ready sat up, feeling his lung slide against his heart and stomach, and took the phone from his mum and held it in the crook of his neck, eyes still closed. "Yeah?"

"Ready?"

"Yeah."

"Ready, I got you a lung. A good one. Someone brought it in this morning. Top of the line. Fresh."

"Fresh?" Ready asked, wondering, and a little concerned, how Surge would acquire an actual, fresh lung.

"You know what I mean. "Fresh". Like nearly new. Only one previous owner, low mileage. Thing looks brand new."

"Where'd you get it?"

"Never mind that. Get down here so I can fit it."

Another surgery so soon after the Deft-skin covering the chunk removed from his side.

"There a kidney with that lung?"

"Nah," Surge said, disappointed. "Kidneys were busted up. Looks like someone took a hammer to the 'bot."

Pieces fell into place and Ready opened his eyes. Ready wanted to nestle back down into sleep, but he could feel his mum's growing impatience at the door.

"I'll see you in an hour," said Ready and hung up.

"You need a lung now?" Joyce muttered as she took the phone from him. Ready wanted to let it go, but knowing his mum would only keep asking he steered the conversation another way.

"I checked over Painswick estate last night. Couldn't find Kenroy, or any sign of him," he said. "Have you heard from Auntie Nia?"

His mother shook her head.

"She called first thing to see if he had turned up here," his mother said. "She thinks he may be out with Sheela Napper's boy."

Ready knew the Nappers, of course. They lived a few blocks over. David Napper, the oldest of Sheela's boys, was in the year above Ready at school. There were four or five younger brothers that followed in alternate years. Every single one of them had gunned for Ready in the years after they dropped out of school. Every. Single. One. If Kenroy was running with a Napper, things were clearly worse than Joyce or Auntie Nia knew.

Ready had heard somewhere that mother's could always tell what their child was thinking, but he believed this was simply not true. His mother had not seen the thoughts that had crossed Ready's face at the mention of the Nappers.

He was tempted to leave Surge's offer until later, but the sensation in his chest was hard to ignore. The slight burn of his organs. The way they seemed to slip over each other. The sensation disturbed Ready.

At the barbershop, Ready took a deep breath and felt the air leave his windpipe and leave his senses as it disappeared into the new metal void newly planted in his chest. The new lung felt larger than his last. Ready felt it tap against his ribs each time he took a breath in.

"You'll get used to it," Surge promised as he put away his equipment and helped Ready up off the table. "It's just a new sound."

It wasn't the sound that bothered Ready, it wasn't even the weight that was considerably more than the BIMEC.

"Have you see Kenroy?" Ready asked as he pulled his t-shirt over his head. "Or any of the Napper boys?"

Surge hesitated. "No," he said. "I haven't seen them."

Ready noted the stiffness Surge spoke with and eyed him with doubt as Surge put the tools into a quick cleaning cycle.

"Surge?" Ready prompted him.

"It's probably nothing," Surge said dismissively, shaking his head and turning his chair away.

"It's probably nothing, but…" Ready encouraged.

Surge rested his chin on his chest, and forced his arms to relax. Ready wasn't going to give up on that slip.

"It *is* probably nothing," Surge said. "I just heard… the Napper, the youngest one, at least, was in here to get a new cut."

"What type of 'cut'?" Ready asked.

Surge turned around and looked at Ready over the top of his glasses. His hands flexed and fell between his thighs. "New job cut."

There was no one around, no one to hear, yet Surge spoke with the same cryptic cues that he would have on the street. Still, Ready understood what was meant by it. A new job cut meant serious business. Indoctrination. On this estate it could only mean one thing.

The worry that Kenroy was following Napper down a dark path was already in his mind, this just confirmed it. The only thing left was to find the boy and determine why Kenroy was prepared to go after Ready.

V

Kenroy waited in the shadow of a concrete column across the road from the chippy next to the corner shops. He tried to stay still, but the compulsion to move was overpowering. He made small steps side to side and allowed his head to bob with each step. He couldn't listen to music; he needed to concentrate, but rather than having thoughts, his inner voice became a radio for his favourite tunes.

He was cold. But, then again, he was always cold. His hands dug down into his pocket as he rocked.

For two days he had been going over the plan. At first he hadn't liked it, but the longer he spent with Napper, the more it made sense. They were right: something had to be done, and it was Kenroy who was in a position to do something. Kenroy was *the* man that could do something about it.

The first part of the plan required knowing Ready's habits, knowing where he'd be and when. That was easy. Anybody on the estate could work that out. The tricky part was getting Ready to lower his guard. Afterall, there was a reason Ready was called Ready.

Friday night. Ready was at the chippy picking up his regular takeaway for Auntie Joyce. Kenroy watched his cousin walk back towards the brutalist block of flats. He was anxious, barely able to keep his skin from shaking with nerves. Goosebumps covered his arms and a charge ran up and down his legs where it sparked at the base of his spine.

Kenroy followed Ready, careful to keep out of sight. No people, no cameras. When Ready was alone, Kenroy whistled to get his attention.

Ready turned, arms out in anticipation, searching out the whistler in the shadows cast from the building.

"Ready!" Kenroy whispered loudly. "Hey, it's me!" He said it as loud as he dared.

Ready looked each way as he crossed over the street.

"Where the fuck have you been?" he demanded to know in a hushed tone, checking around. "Your mum's worried sick."

"I couldn't go home," Kenroy performs his rehearsed line, his eyes darting round from door to door, flinching at every little sound. Ready wasn't the only one watching him closely, he had to pull this off. "I can't be here," Kenroy said, backing off. "I can't."

Ready nodded slowly, stepping towards him. "Let's go," he said.

Kenroy took him to an empty block nearby, one on the western edge of the estate that had been emptied for refurbishment, and the two of them climbed the stairs. Kenroy watched Ready closely. He could hear the scuffle of shoes behind them, but wasn't sure if Ready could hear them too.

Ready bolted. He smashed his way through the fire door at the top of the stairs and rushed out onto the roof, through the concrete mixers and worktools that lay strewn across the rooftop. Kenroy was close behind him, along with Napper and some of the postcode's finest.

Ready had his arms up. His eyes shifted to each of the boys as they stepped forward. Kenroy took a butterfly knife from his pocket and swished it open.

"What are you doing?" Ready demanded to know, glaring at Kenroy. Kenroy was too certain to doubt. Too amped up to back down. "Why are you doing this?"

"You're no man," Kenroy said, stepping forward. The boys beside him stepped forward too. "You're half-bot. You're gonna be one of them."

"A Jackbot?" Ready frowned, lips tensing with disgust and betrayal. "What? You think I would ever be one?"

"I'm here to stop you before you get worse," Kenroy was closing in, just out of arm's reach.

Ready kicked out at his little cousin, his foot thwacking Kenroy in the chest. He was charged from all sides by the boys, pushing them away, breaking skin. Ready's ears pricked up at the sound of others climbing onto the roof. This was Kenroy's initiation. This was his way in. The stupid boy.

Ready brought up his arm to defend himself against a swipe from Kenroy. "You're not a man either," Ready said. "Just a yes-man. A yes-man for the gang. You don't think for yourself, you just do what you're told. Jackbots don't think for themselves and neither do you!"

Kenroy spit blood on the floor beside them. "What are you, then?" He asked. "Jackbot with a face, that's all you are!"

Maybe that was all he was. Maybe that was what he was becoming. But that didn't mean he was going down without a fight.

Ready looked to the door. Looked to the roof edge. But whichever way he looked, there were boys with knives waiting for him.

CAUGHT IN A MOMENT

I am half awake. As always. Drowsy in that groggy mire of waking, unable to drift back off, unable to move. It doesn't happen very often, though of course, it happened today and will keep happening today.

It's not fair that this keeps happening to me. I lose so much time that I could be awake. I start each time with a trembling panic in my chest, unable to open my eyes. Barely able to breathe through my nose – my mouth wired shut by pathways in my mind that haven't woken up.

It takes a moment, it always does, to get my head in gear and be able to sit up in bed. Not that there's any point; I'll be back in it in a moment. I draw the curtain back and let the light flood into my room. The street is silent. It wasn't always. Looking back, the first time people were confused. Some even laughed. A funny prank. Collective déjà vu. An anomaly. Odd. Peculiar even. But something to be laughed off and thought about later – if 'later' ever comes.

This time, when I lean out of my window, the street is deadly silent. People trudge on, or sit, or walk about aimlessly. For the most part it's futile to try and commit to what you were going to do before. What's the point? Unless you were within 90 seconds of your destination, you're never going to get there. Jock in the flat opposite, who has been jogging on that treadmill for what I can only assume is forever, measured the time for me once. That was when we were still talking. I reckon I lose 20-25 seconds each time to the sleep paralysis.

Everyone else gets 90 seconds, and I get more like 65, It's not fair

*

I am half awake. As always. Drowsy in that groggy mire of waking, unable to drift back off, unable to move. It doesn't happen very often, though of course, it happened today and I am sick of it. I work through the suffocating, immobile state and then refuse to move even when I can. I'm not in the mood to move this time. Why would I even bother trying?

I got to the front door once. I sigh. I did get to my front door once; there was no one out there. No one to see or talk to. Maybe other people have tried on different loops, how would I ever know? I wonder what my neighbours are doing. I think upstairs must still be asleep. His bedroom is above mine and I haven't once heard him move. How lucky he is to be unaware of all of this. I don't know if he dreams, but maybe he's revisiting the same portion of his dream. I wonder if you'd ever become aware of that?

The neighbour to my left has already left for work. I know they start early because they usually slam the door on the way out. And to the right is away for the week. I'm supposed to be feeding her fish.

I've not fed her fish in a long, long time. Thinking about it, I haven't had anything to eat either, so I presume the fish is fine.

Huh. If I haven't eaten and I'm not going to eat and I'm no hungrier than I would be waking up in the morning, does that mean that the reset erases everything that happened in the last time? The last loop? I wonder what other people call it? The eternal spin-cycle, the unending marathon. I wonder how far the bloke across the road has run on his treadmill. The treadmill resets. He keeps running. He used to hop off

*

I am half awake. As always. Drowsy in that groggy mire of waking, unable to drift back off, unable to move. It doesn't happen very often, though of course, it happened today and now I'm trying to remember what I was last thinking of?

Across the Road. Treadmill. Running. He used to hop off and come over to the window to chat. Conversations were weird though. Stilted and awkward. Never able to quite get to know each other.

My chest feels heavy. I need to wiggle my toes, but the message isn't getting to them.

How many times have I done this now? How many more times? Am I even ageing? When I can stand up, I'm going to look in the mirror in the bathroom. Maybe do a quick brush of my teeth.

There's no point, I'll reset and I won't have any of the benefits, but I'd like to do something normal, something routine. Something that I would have done if this was going to continue.

Finally, I can stand up. I heave myself out of bed, still stiff and fragile from the paralysis, and make my way through to the bathroom. I probably have about 60 seconds left. I drag myself over to the mirror, wiping crusty sleep from my eyes and look at myself.

Yep. No different.

No different to how I looked yesterday, a thousand cycles ago. Loops ago? I wonder if scientists are doing better at working out what is going on. Imagine if the one person you need to talk to is on the other side of the world, or asleep and when you call them you have to explain over and over again and never get to the point. That would suck.

A shadow flashes past the window. Looks like the third floor has gone back to flinging himself out of the window again. They used to do that regularly. Their white pyjamas flapping in the wind. They cast a darker shadow this time. Maybe they wore a costume, or a bathrobe or something. I remember him saying that if he timed it just right, the sensation of falling and then hitting their bed was quite enjoyable. I'm not sure I would

*

I am half awake. As always. Drowsy in that groggy mire of waking, unable to drift back off, unable to move. It doesn't happen very often, though of course, it happened today and here we go again.

Wait the obligatory amount of time for the paralysis to wear off, then role onto my side and flump off the bed onto the floor. I've probably cracked a rib, but that'll get fixed the moment that I reset. I lie there, facedown, and try to fall back to sleep. I've managed to do it once or twice, but it's not like I'm asleep for a decent amount of time. I end up jolting back up into paralysis.

I turn my head to the side, resting my ear against the carpet. Footsteps. Too loud to be from my downstairs neighbour. Too close to be from a neighbour to either side. Too gentle to be an echo from the outside world.

I've never heard footsteps in a loop.

There's an itch in my lower back. An itch that comes and goes… which is a bit odd now I come to think about it

"Hey!" it's the running man from the flat across the road, shouting at the top of his lungs. "HEY!"

I drag myself up off the ground and go to the window and open it. He hasn't spoken to me in ages. I'm not sure why. We had a falling out, but I can't remember over what. He said something, I said something. I don't suppose it matters.

His arms are flailing about, frantically waving. Gesturing. There are people on the street doing the same thing. Shouting out to me. desperately trying to tell me something. Treadmill man points towards my bathroom. The hallway? The front door?

As I stand, I look through the open bedroom door down the corridor to the front door. The handle is turning

*

I am half awake. As always. Drowsy in that groggy mire of

waking, unable to drift back off, unable to move. It doesn't happen very often, though of course, it happened today and something was different the last time. Something that had never happened before. What was it?

The front door opens. There are shouts from outside. I remember.

I desperately fight off the paralysis as quickly as I can, shaking life into my limbs. It doesn't matter how hard I try. I can't get my arms or legs to move. I can't cry out. My eyes won't open. I am locked inside.

What do I do? What do I do? My mind begs the question as though my body will suddenly answer.

I can hear the movement inside my flat. It's as though the noise were inside my head. It's so loud. It strikes the nerves in my ears. I think it's in the kitchen, knocking the pans about. Plates smash against the floor. Glasses shattering, scattering across the floor.

Get up.

I'm trying. I'm trying. I am trying to get away. But I'm caught. I'm frozen. I can't move. This time I'm not moving at all.

Get up. Get up. GET UP!

It's back in the corridor. I can hear its footsteps move from the smooth kitchen floor to the carpeted hallway.

It's getting frightfully close

*

I am half awake. As always. Drowsy in that groggy mire of waking, unable to drift back off, unable to move. It doesn't happen very often, though of course, it happened today and it's still here. In my room. And I am trapped, unable to move, unable to get out of it. it doesn't matter how much I long to move my fingers, or mumble to wake up my mouth, nothing is working.

It comes over to the bed, rests its soft, papery hands over my nose and mouth and stares me dead in the eye.

TRAPPED

ACKNOWLEDGEMENT

I'd like to thank my family for all their
support and encouragment.

My friends, for their random conversations
that led to half these thoughts.

And most especially my dad, who profreeds everyhtn I right.

ABOUT THE AUTHOR

Author Redacted

Author Redacted was presumably born and has lived. Originally from somewhere and then resided elsewhere. After studying, Redacted worked here and there in several fields, before returning and then moving on to where they are. The experience gained from this informs the stories that have been, and may be, written.

Redacted currently lives, works and writes; fuelled by tea, spite and disapproving looks from a cat.

Can be found on Twitter @r_dact_d

Printed in Great Britain
by Amazon